Diana Marie DuBois

Diana Marie DuBois

Cover Art: Anya Kelleye
www.anyakelleye.com

Published by Three Danes Publishing L.L.C.

Cover art by Anya Kelleye
http://www.anyakelleye.com
Edited by Lisa Angel Miller

Acknowledgements

~My street team Diana's Voodoo Dolls, thank you for all of your pimping skills. You do me proud and I love each and every one of y'all.
~Mary K Henley thanks for all my spells.
~To all mothers out there or in heaven.
~To every daughter who misses their mom, they will forever be in your heart.
~My betas, thank you for loving my stories as much as I do.
~Anita you my dear are the best assistant I could ask for. You have my unending gratitude.
~Lisa thank you for polishing my story.
~Anya thank you for portraying Magnolia Delacroix so perfectly.
~My fans, without you I wouldn't be here still writing my stories.
~ My family who are so proud of me that I was able to accomplish such an enormous task.
~My mother, I love you.

Dedication

To my mama for all you've done for me. You are not only my mother, but my best friend. I wrote this for you and all those times you brushed my hair and sang Chantilly Lace as you put it up in a ponytail. For making me pancakes with peanut butter and homemade maple syrup.

Note to my Readers

The thought of this book came to me when I realized that Rosie's mother was just as important to her, as she was to the series itself. Even though she is not in the book, she is there through Rosie and all the characters. I wanted to show you how important Magnolia Delacroix actually was. As you know, she had an important role in Athena's bond to Rosie as well. The first time I actually gave her a name was in Bred by Magic. Mothers tend to go above and beyond the normal scope of things to protect their daughters, and it made me want to give you more of her. Then, as I wrote Voodoo Vows, I made sure to encompass Magnolia in the little things; in the amulet that Claudette gives her and the voodoo doll from Marie Laveau. So you see, even though Magnolia is not here, she actually is. Even though Rosie thought her mom used the witch "thing", as a ruse to sell stuff in her store, she was the person who groomed and raised Rosie to what she is today. In this story, you will see the witch Magnolia was and the witch Rosie will become, thanks to the memories of her childhood and the years following. I will pull memories from Rosie's childhood, but what you will see is the love of a mother for her daughter. Therefore, for any of you that have lost your mother, remember she is always with you; and if they are still with you, remember, never to take them for granted and always tell them you love them.

Each chapter retells a special memory of Rosie with her mother and Jahane and contains a recipe from her childhood and mine.

Glossary

Bourre – A trick-taking gambling card game primarily played in the Acadiana region of Louisiana.

Bread Pudding (New Orleans Style) – Lightly spiced bread pudding, flavored with bourbon, bourbon sauce, and bourbon-soaked raisins.

Café Dumonde – A famous landmark established in 1862 before the Civil War. Well known for its beignets and café au lait.

Gumbo – Thick, spicy soup prepared with ingredients such as rice, sausage, chicken, and okra.

Holy Trinity – Onions, celery, and bell pepper.

Jackson Square – A historic park in the French Quarter that houses the famous equestrian statue of Andrew Jackson.

Jambalaya – Spicy dish always made with rice and combinations of seafood, chicken, turkey, sausage, peppers, and onions.

Lost Bread – French Toast.

Pecan – A nut indigenous to the South, and beloved in New Orleans as an ingredient in pies and pralines. Pronounced "puh-KAWN," not "PEE-can."

Praline – A sugary Creole candy, invented in New Orleans (not the same as the French culinary/confectionery term "praline" or "praliné") The classic version is made with sugar, brown sugar, butter, vanilla, and pecans, and is a flat sugary pecan-filled disk. There are also creamy pralines, chocolate pralines, maple pralines, etc

Roux - Flour and oil mixture used to start almost all Louisiana dishes.
Ya Mamma – Your mother. Used in a variety of ways, usually endearing. Also usable as an insult, specifically as a simple retort when one is insulted first; simply say, "Ya mamma."
Ya mama'en'em – New Orleans slang for "your mom and them."

Chapters

A mother is like a flower; each one beautiful and unique

~Anonymous

Best Friends Forever

With Jahane and Rosie

1995...age eight

I woke up early and rolled over in bed. My eyes opened to the sunlight peeking through the curtains. I lay there for a few moments and contemplated going downstairs. When I crawled out of my bed and stood in front of the mirror, I stared back at my eight-year-old face. As I rubbed at it, I hoped that one day I would be as beautiful as my mother. All of a sudden, the delicious aroma of pancakes blew up the stairs and into my room. The scent made my stomach growl in anticipation. I padded back over to my bed, knelt down, and looked under it for my slippers. When I found them, I gripped them by the heel, then stuffed my feet into the soft comfortableness. I stood up and headed out of my room. The buttery smell of breakfast gripped my stomach even more, I followed it down the hall and skidded around the corner. I gripped the wall, as I almost tumbled into the kitchen, the whiff of pancakes grew stronger and more intoxicating. By now, my mouth watered and my stomach growled fiercely. The stack of fluffy silver dollars was a welcome sight, as they sat on a plate on the counter.

I glanced around and saw no sign of my mama. Not being able to help myself, I tore a small piece of a pancake from the plate and popped into my mouth. The taste made me want more so I hollered from the kitchen. “Mammmaaaaa, where is the syrup?”

“Rosie, it’s in the fridge.” The sound of my mother’s voice rang through the house. I opened the fridge and the coldness hit me like a breeze on a muggy, summer day. With my head in the fridge, I dug around. When I found the homemade maple syrup in the glass container, I hurried and grabbed it, careful not to let it slip from my hand. I poured some into a small pot and turned on the heat. There was nothing better than warm syrup. On my way to the table, I grabbed the jar of peanut butter. I sat down at the table and began to spread the goopy peanut butter over my pancakes. The smell of maple syrup floated through the house as it bubbled in the pot. I pushed my chair out and went over to the stove. With very careful movements, I poured some of the dark liquid into a cup. The sweet smell hit my senses as I sniffed the maple aroma and headed back to the table where I sat and smothered the stack of buttery delicacy with a heavy dose of syrup.

While I cut my breakfast into little bite sized pieces, mama walked in. "So what do you have planned for today?"

With a mouthful of buttery pancakes and peanut butter, trying to speak was fruitless.

"Ohmmmfr I drmmon't mkrnow, I mrfay frjuust strrfay in mmmryyy frroom and frrread," I replied.

She laughed, as I tried with no luck to lick the gooey substance from the roof of my mouth. "Petal, would you like to help me in the store today? I have a new shipment and I'd love it if my favorite assistant was with me."

I tried once again to answer her, but the glop of peanut butter that was stuck on the roof of my mouth wouldn't budge.

Mama just shook her head at me while I tried to lick the peanut butter off, so I could answer her. Once I had swallowed my bite, I answered. "Sure thing, Mama, just let me get dressed."

After I had finished with breakfast, I put my dishes into the sink with a clatter and ran off to get dressed. Anxious to help down at the store, I threw on a pair of jeans and an old T-shirt. I shoved my feet into my sneakers before sprinting out of my room. I barely noticed the echo of my footfalls on the hardwood floors, as I bounded through the hall and down the back stairs, jumping down them two at a time and heading through the back door, letting it hit the frame with a crack. I hollered as I ran inside. "Mammaaaaa, I'm here. What do you need me to help with first?" I became giddy at the thought of what she had bought. She always had new herbs, trinkets, and new crystal balls. As soon as I entered the shop, I stopped and felt a goofy smile spread across my face at the sight of Miss Alina.

"Miss Alina!" I ran over to her.

My mama's best friend turned to me, as I ran into her warm embrace. "How are you, Rosie?" she asked, as she returned my hug and patted my head.

As I leaned into her warm hug and smelled her usual scent of lavender and magnolias, the door whooshed open and the little bell above the door tinkled and swung back and forth. A young girl about my age skidded in. Her tennis shoes squeaked on the floor, as she stopped suddenly and looked around. Her skin was the color of milk chocolate and her short, black curls bounced in harmony with every step she took.

My mama walked over and asked, "How may I help you, dear?"

"Yes ma'am..."

Her big brown eyes stared up at my mother and she glanced back over at me, from where I was peeking out from beside the counter. She nodded at me and her curls again bounced with her head.

She scanned the room and turned back to my mom. "Uh, ma'am, what kind of a store is this?" she asked.

Before my mom could answer, she looked around her and stared again at me. "Hey, haven't I seen you around school? You are the new girl, the one who always has a book with you, right? What's your name?" Her slew of questions sent my head spinning. With a smile on her face, my mother stood back and watched the two of us.

My head moved up and down. "Yes, but I haven't been at school for long, I just got there. And uh, my name is Rosie Delacroix," I stammered, not sure about this pushy girl.

"What's yours?" I inquired.

She walked over to me and held out her hand. "I am Jahane Olivier, and maybe you and I could be friends." She winked at me, and as she batted her eyelashes, I instantly warmed to her, recognizing a budding friendship in the making.

I shook her hand. She looked nice and seemed genuine about being friends. "Sure, thing, Jahane," I replied, "let's be friends."

I turned my head to look at my mama. "Mama, I know you wanted me to help you in the store, but maybe Jahane and I could play together today?" I asked.

"Oh, Petal, I don't mind, but shouldn't Jahane call her mom and make sure it's ok."

I turned to Jahane. "Do you want to stay and play? You could use our phone."

My mother's inviting smile lingered as Jahane seemed to ponder the idea of staying. "Come along, dear, I'll show you the phone."

When Jahane hung up the phone with a smile plastered on her face, I knew we would be spending the day together. "My mom said I could stay until supper time."

"Awesome, come on then. We can play up in my room." We ran off in a whirlwind of giggles. The back door thwacked against the doorframe as we ran outside and up the wooden stairs to my apartment. "Come on in, this is my room."

Jahane walked around and then plopped down on the round, pink rug in the middle of my room, crossed her legs, and looked up at me.

"So, Rosie, what do you want to do?"

I sat across from her. "Um well, we could play some games; maybe a board game or some cards." I smiled over at her.

"Ok, whatcha got in mind?" she asked.

"Hmmm, have you ever heard of Bouree?" I inquired.

She seemed intrigued at my game idea. "No, what is that?"

"It's a card game I used to play with the neighbors down the bayou," I told her.

"Ooh, I'm game. Can you teach me how to play?" She giggled.

I nodded. "I sure can. Wait, we need something." I grabbed the piggy bank from my desk and emptied it on the floor, grabbing the ones that rolled under my bed.

With all the pennies splayed out on the floor, I sat back down across from her and dealt us five cards each.

"Ok, this I how you play." I turned over the last card I dealt myself face up on the floor. "Hearts are trumps. Keep all of your hearts and if you want, you can discard some of yours in the hopes of getting more trump cards."

She looked at me and shuffled through her cards. "Here, Rosie." She placed all her cards face down on the floor. I dealt out five more cards to her, and then looked at my own hand.

"Now if you have a high card, play that one, if not, play a card that goes over that five of hearts."

She looked at her cards. "But, Rosie, I don't have any hearts."

I giggled. "Okay this hand doesn't count so I can show you how to play." I scooted over and peeked at her hand. Knowing I had all hearts, I told her to play her two of spades. When she placed it down on the floor I said, "Okay, since I had the five of hearts and you had a two of spades, I won that trick."

She smiled at me and thumbed through her other cards. Finally, she picked one and placed it down. "How about an ace of spades?"

I quirked a brow at her and glanced at my cards. I picked a two of hearts and placed if over her card. "Now, because I have a heart and you don't, I win this trick too. Even if your card is bigger, mine is a trump."

After a few more tries, she figured out how to play. We started playing for pennies we divvied up them up evenly between us. We went back and forth, both making each other bouree, but after a while we needed more things to put in the pot.

"What are we going to use now?" she asked.

"Jahane, I know what we can use." I giggled.

"You do?" she cocked a brow at me.

"Yes, come on." I grabbed her hand and we ran downstairs giggling.

My mother and Miss Alina turned around when we both came around the corner and skidded to a halt right in front of her. "What is it girls?" my momma asked.

When I caught my breath, I sputtered out, "Do we have any pecans left?"

"Why, Rosie, what in the world do you want pecans for?" She crossed her arms over her chest and smiled with a sense of what we were up to.

"Uh well, yeah hmm, we decided to play Bouree, and we ran out of pennies." I stifled a giggle.

"Oh, Magnolia, let them have a few. We still have plenty to make the pralines." Miss Alina smiled down at me and cocked a brow, knowing I would be intrigued and want to help make pralines.

"Mama, do you think we could help make some pralines. Puhleeeeeeeeeese," I begged.

The two exchanged glances and smiled. Both Jahane and I sucked in a breath while we waited for them to say we could help. After what seemed like an eternity, they both nodded and we jumped up and down with exuberance. "But, before you do, could ya'll unload the new boxes that arrived today, for us? Please be careful of the breakable items girls."

"Yes ma'am," we sputtered out in unison as we ran back to the storeroom to unpack the boxes.

Jahane and I opened box after box. "Rosie, what is all this stuff?"

I pulled a crystal ball out of the box and smiled at her. "Oh, my mama sells these items to the tourists," I bent down and whispered low in her ear, "They think she is a witch." Jahane popped back up and quirked a brow at me, shaking her head in disbelief. Carefully we emptied the boxes one by one. Each time we emerged from the back, Mama instructed where to put the items. Once we were finished and all the new merchandise was displayed on the shelves, I stepped back and looked at my new friend. "Hey, it looks like we make a good team."

"I think so too." We high fived each other and plopped down on the sofa, exhausted.

"Looks like they may be too tired to make pralines," I heard momma tell Miss Alina.

"I agree, Magnolia."

We jumped up as if the springs from the sofa had propelled us and ran over to the counter. "No, we are fine," we said in unison. "All right, girls, head upstairs and wash your hands and Alina and I will be up in a moment," Mama told us while she flipped the 'out to lunch' sign and turned the lock on the front door of the shop.

We raced outside, through the courtyard, and up the stairs two at a time, and scrambled into the bathroom. When we came out, I showed my new bestie the apartment and we made our way to the kitchen. I pulled back one of the barstools and sat alongside Jahane. We sat at the counter and swung our feet back and forth while we waited for my mama and Miss Alina.

"So, you are new here, huh?" she asked.

"Yes, we've been here for about a year, but came mid-school season, so momma just let me sit out and start at the new school year."

"Did you have trouble catching up?" she questioned.

"No, not really. I was ahead of my class back in my hometown. What they were learning, I'd already learned."

When my mama walked in, we were deep in conversation about school and what classes we had in common. She walked towards the stove, her skirt twirling almost magically with every movement she made.

I looked up and noticed she was alone. "Mama, where is Miss Alina?"

"Oh, she had to head back to her shop, dear Petal. Besides, she thought it would be ok that I help you and Jahane make pralines." Her smile crinkled the outer corners of her eyes.

We both waited excitedly for our instructions from her while we watched her get out all the supplies and ingredients to make the most delicious, sugary, concoction known to man. "Rosie, go and grab two aprons out of the pantry for you and Jahane."

"Yes ma'am." I opened the door and pulled two aprons off the hook on the back. I handed one of them to Jahane.

Once we donned our aprons and had wooden spoons in hand, we were ready. My eyes lit up when she poured the two different sugars into the pan. It seemed almost magical; she even hummed a little tune that I couldn't quite make out. She stirred together the regular sugar with the brown sugar and evaporated milk with her own wooden spoon. She stirred and stirred until the sugar had dissolved. The air around us looked shiny and silvery as she continued her song.

This and that to combine and mix.
A little lesson to teach some tricks.
Whatever you do remember to add love.
And your outcome certain to be proud of.

After she finished she turned to face me, let go of the spoon for a split second, and I swear it dipped itself and mixed the sugary concoction by itself. I stood there shocked, blinked my eyes once, twice, and glanced up at her as she winked at me.

"Rosie, can you and Jahane get the baking sheets ready with wax paper? Before you do, can you grab the candy thermometer for me?"

"Yes ma'am," I replied, handing her the thermometer.

She stirred the mixture until, "All right, girls, the candy is ready, so bring me the butter and pecans."

She removed the pot from the burner and we both grabbed a bowl of toasted pecans. I turned around and scooped up the small plate with sticks of butter that we quickly cut into little chunks. I handed mama the butter and watched while she dropped the pats on top. We both watched the little yellow squares slowly get sucked into the sugar until they disappeared. The minutes we waited for it to finish felt like an eternity. After a few minutes, Mama took the vanilla and poured two tsp in. She nodded at me to bring the pecans and I poured them into the rest of the concoction. She began to stir smoothly until it turned a light caramel color. Once the candy began to get thicker, we knew it was almost ready. Mama dipped the wooden spoon in and out to see if the candy held its shape, when it did, she quickly started to drop small dollops onto the wax paper. The smell of sugar and pecans fanned through the small apartment. Almost instantly, Jahane and I couldn't wait to taste what we had made. Trust me, thirty minutes was a long time to wait.

After getting two glasses of milk, we sat back on the barstools, impatiently swinging our legs back and forth. “Mama, is it almost ready?”

“Almost, Petal.” She turned and stepped into the pantry to grab more pecans.

While she was out of sight and before they were cooled, I couldn’t wait any longer, so I scooped two of the warm pralines onto napkins. I whispered, “Here, try this,” and handed one to Jahane. I bit into mine and the sugar exploded in my mouth like a confectioners dream. I savored every saccharine bite. My attention turned to the ooohs and ahhs coming from the girl next to me. When I glanced in Jahane’s direction, she was popping the last bite in her mouth. My mother walked back in just as we finished. She laughed as she noticed the two empty spots on the wax paper.

“Come on, girls; let’s make a few more batches, that way Jahane can take some home to her family.” She smiled as we jumped down off the stools we were perched on and washed our hands again.

My mother began to mix the ingredients and Jahane and I took turns pouring the pecans and mixing everything together. Once we had made more, we bagged them up and set some aside for Jahane to take home when it was time. After we helped mama wash the dishes, we grabbed a few pralines and headed back to my room.

“Wow, you sure do have a lot of books.” She sounded astonished.

I laughed, "Yes, my mama always said reading was important."

"Can I borrow one?"

"Sure you can. Which one would you like to read?" I asked.

She thumbed through the books and picked one she seemed to be interested in. "Here, I'll try this one."

"Ohh, you picked a good one Jahane. Dracuuuuuuula," I said in my best scary impersonation and waved my hands in the air. "Are you sure you won't be scared?" I joked.

"Pfft, I am descended from Marie Laveau herself," she replied.

I looked at her in astonishment. "Are you for real or are you pulling my leg?"

She nodded and sat down next to me with the book in her hand. "Yep, I sure am. We come from a long line of voodoo priestesses."

Before I could ask her anything else, I heard my mama's voice outside the door. "Rosie, Jahane's mother is here to pick her up."

I glanced over in Jahane's direction. "Jahane, can you come back tomorrow after school so we can hang out?" I inquired.

She looked at me and nodded her head. "Of course, we are best friends now." She jumped off the bed and her curls bounced up and down. With that, she smiled and we ran into the living room, giggling the whole way. We stopped when saw her mother and mine talking.

"I hope she wasn't a bother," I heard her ask my mama.

"No, she was a perfect angel. They got along fine and clicked instantly." My mother turned to us as she noticed us walk in. "Rosie, come meet Mrs. Kellette Olivier, Jahane's mother."

I walked over to her. "It's nice to meet you, ma'am," I said, and offered my hand. She accepted it and smiled down at me.

She turned to Jahane. "So, did you girls have fun today?" she asked.

My new best friend nodded her head, glanced over to me and we giggled, as if we already had a secret language.

Jahane's mom placed an arm around her daughter. "Well, Magnolia said you are welcome to come back any time to play with Rosie."

Before they left, Jahane ran over to me and hugged me tight. "See you tomorrow, bestie." My mother handed Jahane her bag of pralines and hugged her goodbye as well.

Later that night while my mama brushed my long, dark hair, she hummed my favorite song, 'Chantilly Lace', and asked. "So, Rosie, did you and Jahane have fun today? She seems like a nice girl."

I nodded. "Yes ma'am. She said we are best friends. And, Mama, I'm glad she came into the store today."

My mother just nodded and smiled. "Me too. Me too, my little Petal."

⚜⚜⚜⚜

She continued to pass the brush through every strand down the length of my silky hair. She continued singing and I giggled at her out of tune rendition of the song she always sung at this time.

"My little Petal, are you laughing at my singing voice," she inquired.

"No, Mama." I covered my face as I tried to stifle a laugh. "But, Mama" I giggled, as I said, "my favorite part is coming up."

"Ahhhh" and she began to sing again . . .

We both began to sing into hairbrushes and dance and shake around the room until we collapsed on the bed in a fit of giggles. I rolled over, wrapped my arms around her, and hugged her tight. "I love you, Mama."

"I love you too, my Petal."

Pralines

Pralines are a New Orleans institution! In the first chapter, the reason I picked this recipe is because all young kids like to help their moms make candy or cookies. This praline recipe produces sweet, slightly crumbly, brown sugar candies loaded with toasted pecans. It's important that the pecans be well toasted so that they impart maximum flavor and crunch to the candy.

Ingredients:

1 cup granulated sugar
1 cup packed brown sugar
1/2 cup evaporated milk
4 tbsp butter, cubed
2 tsp vanilla extract
1.5 cups toasted pecans, coarsely chopped

Preparation:

Prepare a baking sheet by lining it with wax paper foil and spraying the foil with nonstick cooking spray.
In a medium saucepan, combine the brown sugar, granulated sugar, and evaporated milk over medium heat. Stir until the sugar dissolves, then insert a candy thermometer.

Cook the candy, stirring occasionally, until the candy reaches 240 degrees on the thermometer.

Once the proper temperature is reached, remove the pan from the heat and drop the chunks of butter on top, but do not stir. Allow the pan to sit for one minute.

After a minute, add the vanilla extract and the pecans, and begin to stir smoothly and constantly with a wooden spoon. Soon the candy will begin to get thicker and lighter in color.

Continue to stir until the candy starts to hold its shape. It should still be easy to stir, however. It is important not to stir too much, as pralines quickly go from fluid to rock-solid. Once it is a lighter, opaque brown and holds its shape, quickly begin to drop small dollops of the candy onto the prepared baking sheet.

Work quickly to form the candies, as the pralines will start to set in the saucepan. If the candy stiffens before you're done scooping, add a spoonful of very hot water and stir until it loosens, then continue scooping until you have formed all the pralines. Allow the candy to set fully at room temperature for about 30 minutes. Store your pralines in an airtight container at room temperature.

Tragedy Makes You Stronger

With Everyone

2002... age fifteen

One day as I walked home after spending the day at Miss Alina's, I stopped at Café Dumonde to pick up some beignets for my mama as a surprise. With the little white bag in hand, I stopped at the intersection. After I had looked both ways, I began to cross the street. I heard a commotion further down near the Square. I turned my head at all the noise and saw a mule barreling down the street, the carriage bouncing and being dragged behind him. As it got closer, I could see its nostrils flare.

"Young lady, watch out! Get out of the way!" The crowd and the driver yelled. I froze in the middle of the street, fear enveloping me as I stood there, unable to move. My earthshattering scream became muffled by the pain I felt when the mule, and then the wheel of the carriage, rolled over my thigh.. As I hit the pavement with a thud, I heard screams off in the distance to call 911. I felt the blacktop cut into my back as I lay there, unable to move. "Why me, why did this happen?" I thought. The mule struggled, but from what I could see in my haze, someone had a hold of him. My leg hurt so bad I wanted to scream. I tried, but no sound came from my mouth. Wet warmth began to cover my leg and seep all around me. I flailed my arms to move, but the rest of me was cemented to the blacktop.

I heard a voice trying to calm the mule and me down, "Shhhh, young lady, don't move please."

I felt another person lean down beside me and wipe the hair from my face. The gruff male voice spoke. "You'll be fine, don't move. Everything will be okay."

"But, sir...I...can't...mo..." I managed to get out through sobs.

"Just hang tight," the man told me.

The voice became muffled and I could barely make out what had been said as he moved away from me and spoke to the other man. I drifted in and out, but tried to listen to what they were saying.

"Oliver, if we don't get this wheel off of her she will lose her leg."

"I know Louis, but we need to unhook the carriage from the mule so he doesn't pull on it anymore."

At the thought of me losing my leg, I tried to move, but was held down by someone, probably the man named Louis, but I couldn't focus on him. Fear held me tight in its grip and I wanted my mama. Then everything went dark.

"Rosie, Rosie!" The sound of my mama's panicky voice rang in my head and made me try to open my eyes.

I blacked out right before the EMT's arrived. The pain came and went, and when I regained consciousness, I heard the sound of a male's hushed voice. I strained my ears to hear what he said, but at that precise moment, a needle pricked my arm, my body relaxed, and I was out cold.

The sound of continuous beeps woke me. I opened my eyes and realized I couldn't feel anything below my waist. A sudden panic erupted and my breathing became hurried. "Mama, where are you?"

I tried to move but couldn't. Once I calmed down, I looked around and saw many machines. I heard noises outside the room, the sound of someone yelling, but I couldn't tell what was being said, only that they were mad. Then the door opened and my best friend peeked around the door. She tiptoed in and my heart leapt at the site of her. As she inched closer, I saw the tears in her eyes and just couldn't deal with that right now, so I closed my eyes and pretended to sleep. I felt Jahane sit down next to me and brush my hair away from my face. A tear slid down my face and hit the pillow.

"I'm here for you, bestie, and always will be."

As I drifted back to sleep, I hoped she told the truth.

⚜⚜⚜⚜

When I woke later, I glanced around the room and noticed an extra bed in my room. I knew it could only be one person....my bestie. I knew I was right when my eyes focused on her ebony curls sprawled across the pillow. I looked over to my right and could feel her presence without even a glance at her. My mother had her arm draped over my body. When she felt me stir, she looked up at me and her red-rimmed eyes broke my heart.

"Oh, my precious, Petal, I thought I had lost you." She cried softly.

I wiped the tears that had begun to fall from my eyes. "I'm sorry, Mama."

"Oh, my darling daughter, you have no reason to be sorry. It was just an accident." She wiped her face, as a tear trickled down to land on her chin.

"What happened, Mom?" I croaked out.

"Oh, Petal, don't worry about that now," she said, trying to comfort me. She held my hand as if she never wanted to let go. She began to whisper something I couldn't quite make out.

"What, Mama?" I asked.

She smiled down at me. "It's nothing to worry your head about. Now, why don't you get some sleep? I know Alina will be by later to visit you."

I nodded and rolled back over, smiling as Jahane's eyes sluggishly opened. She mouthed, "Hi bestie, get some rest."

I smiled back at her and closed my eyes.

After what felt like a few hours, though I knew it had not been long, I woke to the sound of the doctors talking to my mom. I looked around for my best friend, but I didn't see her anywhere. With as much effort as I could muster, I tried to sit up just a bit. A nurse bustled over to check my vitals and her warm smile made me feel safe. I tried once again to hear what the doctor told my mom. I heard the doctor say, "Ms. Delacroix, we've stopped the bleeding and maintained her heart rate, but we need to perform the surgery today or she will lose the leg."

"Do what you need to," I heard her reply, then she came over to me and sat down in the chair beside my bed.

"Good, I will set up the OR and we will prep her." Before the doctor left, he gave me a smile of reassurance.

My eyes followed the doctor out, and when the door closed behind him, my gaze returned to the face of my mother. "My Petal, how are you feeling?" Her voice was laced with concern, as she grabbed my hand.

My voice was barely audible and hoarse. I croaked out, "I am ok I guess, just tired."

"Get some rest, honey. You will have surgery in a few hours." She kissed me on the nose and tucked a strand of lose hair behind my ear. Within moments, I fell fast asleep.

I heard hushed voices in my room. With my eyes still closed, I was gently moved from my bed to a gurney. The move from my room to the operating room held a vague sensation to me. I knew I headed down the long hallway, but drowsiness overtook me.

⚜⚜⚜⚜

Once my surgery had been done, I woke to a room full of balloons and flowers. I still couldn't move my leg, which worried me. Soon, my self-pity was interrupted by the sound of my best friend.

"Rosie!" she squealed out, as she rushed into the room. In her excitement, she almost let the door shut in her mom's face.

"Jahane, young lady, be careful." Her mother chastised her. Her smile was void of pity, only full of love and concern. "I hope you are feeling better, Rosie," she said, before heading over to speak to my mama.

"Yes ma'am," I squeaked out.

"Omg, Rosie!" Jahane's voice pulled me back to her. She hugged me tight and gasped. "Oh gosh, I didn't hurt you, did I?"

I laughed. "Uh no, my arms are not hurt, just my leg."

"I'm so glad you will be all right." She sat on the edge of the bed and looked at me, whispering, "I overheard the doctor talking to your mom. They said you will be okay." She smiled and wiped at a tear that slid down her cheek. "I just don't know what I would do if I'd lost my bestie."

I grinned at her. "I think you are stuck with me." The instant I became surrounded by Jahane I felt better.

There also seemed to be something else in the room, almost like a calming effect, and that is when I noticed her. Miss Alina stood over to the side of the room waving a stick that smelled oddly familiar. The smell of sage overpowered the room, but the thick smoke dissipated quickly. She mouthed, "It's for cleansing."

I nodded at her. She nodded back at me and moved to another section of the room, waving the stick over there.

My mother came to sit beside me on the bed. I noticed that Mrs. Olivier now stood by Miss Alina. They both smiled over at me. I turned my attention back to my mama as she sat on the opposite edge of the bed as Jahane and recited a little poem to me.

Once a young girl
Her strength was strong
But in a whirl
Things went wrong.
Hidden spell that has been untold

Hear my words loud and bold
Look to her future that's still so long
Change the time, fix the wrong
Transform her weakness and make her once again strong

With the words spoken from my mother and the family I had in the room, I became instantly calm and knew things would be ok.

Every day Jahane went with my mom and me to physical therapy. Even at fifteen, Jahane was still pushy and boy crazy. "Oh, Rosie, your physical
therapist is too fine." Her last word drawled out for emphasis.

I shook my head as I hobbled in on crutches, trying not to look at Cole Scott, my sexy therapist, as Jahane had put it. I swooned the moment he looked over at me and smiled.

"Good morning, Rosie." I swayed a bit and Jahane caught me without anyone knowing I'd almost
toppled over.

"See what I'm talking about. Fine with a capital F," she breathed out, as she held me upright.

"Hi, Cole," I stuttered out and turned to Jahane, giving her my best *stop embarrassing* me look.

She harrumphed, as she flounced over to a chair and picked up a magazine. As the weeks passed, I went through a lot of physical therapy, but was told that with lots of hard work, I would walk again.

⚜⚜⚜⚜

The weeks that followed were tough, but I got through them with my family and friend by my side. Slowly, my leg healed, though the jagged scars were visible to everyone, so I began to wear long skirts to cover up my legs.

When I returned to school, I still had a slight limp. One day, I stood leaning against my locker waiting for Jahane to come out of class. Down the hall, some of the high school football team walked my way and stopped in front of me. I dropped my head and pretended to fiddle with my fingernail.

"Oh, Rosie..."

I looked up to catch one sneering down at me. I huddled closer to my locker, hoping to melt into it. One of them put both of their arms on either side of me and held his face inches away from me. He opened his mouth to speak and the sweet smell of cherry bubble gum oozed out on his breath. "Rosie, why didn't they just cut off your leg, I think you'd have been better off with a peg leg, don't you boys?" He turned to look at his cohorts. They all laughed and slapped each other on the back at his joke.

I held back the tears and just stared back at him, not muttering a single word.

"What, now you are mute and can't speak. Did they cut out your tongue instead?" He laughed even harder. Just as Jahane came out of the class, one of the boys pushed me down. I skidded across the tile floors away from my locker. As I did, my skirt flew up enough to reveal my scars. I quickly pushed my skirt down and held my legs close to my chest.

"Rosie, what in the world!" She raced over to me and helped me up.

"They attacked me."

"I know." When she had me up she looked from me to them. I turned my face away to wipe the falling stream of tears from my face. She walked over to them and in a low, deep voice, I heard her say, "If you boys ever come near Rosie again, I... oh hell, I swear I will put a voodoo curse on you."

"Oh, crap!" I heard them exclaim and scramble to get away from both of us as fast as they could. Their shoes squeaked along the floor as they ran. I turned my tear stained face back just in time to see the last boy run headfirst into the wall, and bounce off of it and slam into the floor. Jahane did not hide her laughter, as she guffawed rather loudly. "I mean it!" she yelled, as the last guy rounded the corner.

She turned to me and dusted her hands off. "Come on, Rosie, I know how we can fix those idiots." With that, she grabbed my arm and led me out of the school building.

"Where are we going?" I questioned.

"First we need to get some money. Do you have any?"

I nodded, as we caught the streetcar back to my apartment in the Quarter. We ran the whole way up the steps in silence. Once in my room, I emptied my piggy bank onto the floor. We scraped all the loose change into a baggie and ran out. As we left my courtyard, I stopped her and asked, "Okay, now tell me where we are going."

"You'll see." She still had a grip on my hand when we arrived back at the streetcar.

We hopped on the streetcar and took our seats. The ride was a quick one, though I had enough time to contemplate what had just happened. Once we had arrived at our destination, I looked around. "Jahane, what are we doing here." I looked up at the sign that hung above the door and read 'The Loa Voodoo Shop.'

"We are here to cast our revenge on those that dare to hurt my bestie." She cackled, in her best scary voice.

I rolled my eyes at her as she stepped inside the shop. I followed her, but as I walked around the store, the tiny hairs on the back of my neck stood on end. I shivered, not from cold, but from fear. I didn't want to be here; this store seriously put off a heavy dose of the creep factor.

My gaze followed Jahane's steps around the store. I felt another chill run up and down my spine as a short, old man walked out from behind the counter, leaning on a wooden cane. I hadn't even seen him, and I almost jumped and screamed. In fact, I did scream the moment I felt a hand on my arm.

I looked over at the hand on my arm. "Geez Jahane, give me a heart attack why don't you?"

She shook her head. "Why are you so jumpy, Rosie?"

We turned our attention back to the creepy little man who stood before us, with a look of disgust on his wrinkled face.

"Can I help you girls?"

Jahane nodded. "Yes sir. We need a voodoo doll. You see, my best friend has been dealing with bullies at school and I want to fix them up."

The creepy little man nodded and then his eyes changed colors. I blinked, thinking I was seeing things. "Are you planning on speaking with any of the loa? What kind of spells are you planning on doing?"

"Oh, I don't know," Jahane replied, now fidgeting. "Who are the loa?" she inquired.

"Oh, little girl, if you don't know who they, are then you certainly don't need to speak with them." He smirked.

Jahane and I linked arms and she shrugged. "Yes sir, I just need to get back at a bunch of boys who messed with my best friend."

"Well, let's see what I have over here. I think these items will be just what you need."

As we followed him, he picked out a few things. He would stop and ponder on an object and either shake his head or grab the item from the shelf. After fifteen minutes, he had a voodoo doll, some pins, and a few dozen chicken bones in his hand. He placed them on the counter and then shuffled off and picked a few other items. He rang up our items and placed them in a bag.

"That'll be twenty-five dollars." He held out his decrepit hand.

Jahane dug around in her backpack for the baggie of change. She dumped the contents out and they scattered across the counter. The man looked unimpressed and pursed his lips in aggravation. Jahane quickly counted out the exact change and shoved the rest back into the baggie. "Here you go, sir," she said, as politely as she could.

He took the change and popped it into the cash register. We grabbed the bag and headed over to Jahane's house in Treme'.

⚜⚜⚜⚜

We stood on her front porch and I nervously grabbed her arm. "Are you sure your mama isn't home?" I asked.

"Yup." She bobbed her head up and down.

The door creaked, as we entered her little shotgun house. I followed her all the way to the back of the house to her room. We sat crossed legged on her bed; my hand absentmindedly traced the design on her quilt, as she laid out all of our stuff. Picking up the items, I looked at them and shook my head at Jahane as she smiled over at me. Suddenly, she pulled a piece of hair out of her pocket.

"Where did you get that?" I inquired.

"When I made the boys almost pee themselves." She laughed.

I watched her intently as she mixed together the items we had bought and placed them all a little bag. Before she could utter the words of the spell, the door flew open. Mrs. Olivier walked into the room, and when she saw what we were up to, her face lit up with anger.

"Jahane Elizabeth Olivier and Rosaleigh Delacroix, what is the meaning of this?" Her voice got louder, as she scanned the items on the bed.

"But..but...Mama, we were just trying to get back at some kids at school," she stammered.

"No! Jahane, we don't mess with voodoo, it's a dangerous thing to play with, especially if you do it wrong. The loa don't like it when children use it for such trivial reasons."

Jahane stood from the bed and took on a defiant tone, one I knew she would be in trouble for later, after I left. "But the kids were teasing my Rosie and I wanted to teach them a lesson."

The look she gave her daughter was one of disappointment and anger. She came over to me and her look was full of concern as she sat on the bed. She took my now shaking hand and patted it. "Rosie, I know you are hurting right now, but it will get better. You can't let the kids get to you."

I pulled my hand away to wipe my face. Tears filled my eyes and began to flow, dropping onto my hands that were now crossed in my lap. I held my head down in shame. "I know, ma'am. But it hurts so much when they pick on me."

"Oh, sweetie." Jahane's mother wrapped her arms around me and patted my back in comfort.

I leaned into her soft embrace and cried tears of pain.

"Rosie, you do know that these scars do not define you." I bowed my head again, full of embarrassment. She tilted my head up and looked at me. "Don't ever let anyone get to you like this. Those that do not like you because of this aren't worth it. Rosie, you go on now and see your mother. I need to have a talk with Jahane."

I looked over to her to say I was sorry. She ran over to me, hugged me tight, and whispered in my ear, "I would do it again without a doubt. You are my bestie and I would do anything for you."

I sniffed a little at the words from my best friend and hugged her back. "Thanks, I'll see you at school tomorrow." I knew she would probably be grounded for a couple of weeks at least.

⚜⚜⚜⚜

I slowly climbed the stairs and opened the door. Apprehension wrapped around me, as I slowed my pace when I stepped into the apartment. My mom was sitting on the sofa reading a very large book. "Mom, what is that?" I tried to focus her attention on something else before I told her what happened.

She closed the book with a thud. I tried to get a glance at it, but she stood and walked over to me. "What's wrong, Petal?"

As the words tumbled out of my mouth, my mama held me tight. She pulled back and spoke. "Come on, Rosie, let's make your favorite dish." I nodded my head and followed her into the kitchen. My mother was the best cook I knew and I hoped to learn all I could from her. I watched my mom pull out pots and pans, so I walked towards her. “Can I help, Mama?”

“Sure, grab the holy trinity.”

I nodded and began to grab the green stalks of celery, one green bell pepper, and some onions. Mom and I worked in perfect sync. After the sausage and chicken had been cut up, I scraped it off the cutting board and into the cast iron pot. Mama came over to me and put her arms around me. “You know we still need to have a talk about the whole voodoo curse you and Jahane tried to do.”

I nodded, knowing she was disappointed. She squeezed my shoulders and smiled. After about an hour, Mama and I finished cooking the gumbo. The smells in the kitchen floated through and made my mouth water at the thought of eating this delicious meal. I promptly began setting the table. I carried the French bread and butter and placed it on the table as Mama brought two bowls of the steaming gumbo. Silently, I scooped my spoon in and waited for Mama to speak.

Finally, after a few spoonfuls, she placed her spoon down and raised a brow at me. “Now, Petal, what were ya’ll thinking?”

I shook my head, “Well, Jahane wanted to get back at the boys who were mean to me today. So I grabbed all my money from my piggy bank and we headed over to the voodoo shop.”

"Uh huh. Well, I am certain that Mrs. Kellette told you, voodoo is not something to mess with, correct?"

I planned my next sentence carefully and took a bite of gumbo before I answered her. "I know, Mama, but they deserved it. They were mean and said horrible things to me."

"Petal, this world is cruel and you must learn to overcome your tragedy. Never let the issues of other people affect you. Over time, your scars will only make you stronger."

I nodded and finished the last bite of my gumbo. "Yes ma'am," I mumbled through tears.

"Now, if you are done, please pick up your dishes and place them in the sink. After you do the dishes, off to your room to contemplate what you and Jahane have done. I think it's only fair you have the same punishment as her. You will be grounded for two weeks and you and Jahane will not see each other in that time, understood?"

"Yes ma'am," I said, as got up from the table to remove my dishes. After I had washed the dishes and put them away, I walked over to her and hugged her tight. "I'm sorry, Mama." I turned away from her and wiped away the falling tears. I hated that she was disappointed in me.

File Gumbo

Growing up in Louisiana, Gumbo is a staple when it is cold. I always consider it a comfort food as well, so for Rosie and her mother to make this after a bad day at school, just fit together like a puzzle. Gumbo is a Louisiana soup or stew, which reflects and blends the rich cuisines of regional Indian, French, Spanish, and African cultures. The word "gumbo" is derived from the African term for okra, "gombo," and first appeared in print in 1805. Filé gumbo, a version thickened with filé powder (ground sassafras leaves) as used by the Choctaw Indians, came along about 20 years later.

There are no hard and fast rules for making gumbo beyond the basic roux, okra, or filé powder, and your imagination. There are probably as many distinctive recipes for gumbo as there are cooks in Louisiana.

First you make a roux......

The fat used in roux may be butter, shortening, lard, oil, or even bacon drippings. Combine fat with an equal amount of flour ; 1/2 cup of each will make a good amount and any excess can be stored in the refrigerator. (Many cookbooks call for a little more fat than flour - 2/3 cup oil to 1/2 cup flour is a common ratio.) Melt the fat in a black skillet over low heat. When warm and fluid, sprinkle the flour in a little at a time, stirring. Stir constantly until brown (this may take 20 to 30 minutes); immediately remove from heat or add the ingredients your recipe calls for. If it burns even slightly, throw it out and start over again.

Ingredients:

1/2 cup vegetable oil
1/2 cup flour
1 pound smoked sausage
1 1/2 cups chopped onions
1/4 cup chopped green bell peppers
1 cup chopped celery
3 tablespoons butter
1 can (14.5 ounces) diced tomatoes
1 teaspoon black pepper, or to taste
1/2 teaspoon crushed red pepper, or to taste
2 to 4 cloves garlic, minced
2 teaspoons file
A bay leaf
1 teaspoon chili powder
1 teaspoon dried leaf thyme
2 quarts chicken broth
2 cups diced cooked chicken
Salt to taste

Preparation:

In another saucepan, sauté sausage, onions, green and red bell peppers, and celery in butter for approximately 10 minutes; add tomatoes. Stir in roux and seasonings and let simmer for 20 minutes. Slowly stir in chicken broth and simmer for 1 to 1 1/2 hours. Adjust with water or chicken stock to taste. Add chicken and then serve over hot rice. Makes about 1 gallon. Serves 8 to 10.

A chance meeting

Everyone

2011... age twenty-four

Jahane and I sat in the crowded amp theater along with a few dozen tourists. We always loved watching the shows, especially on such a beautiful, sunny day. After the show, we headed back to the shop. Before we crossed the street, a tall guy with long, dark hair bumped into me, almost knocking me down. When he caught me, my breath hitched as his dark, green eyes bore into me. "Excuse me, Miss, I am sorry," he said with me still in his muscular arms.

Staring up at him like a lovesick little girl, I quickly gained my composure and pushed off his chest. As my hands touched him, I tried not to gasp as his muscles flexed under my touch. "It's all right."

As he righted me, I heard Jahane say, "watch out where you going." However, I saw a smile light up her face, as she said it. I knew I wouldn't hear the end of this for a long time.

Before I turned around, Mister *sex on a stick* spoke. "My name is Julian. What's yours?" He smiled and my legs almost gave way.

Jahane dragged me away and over my shoulder, I returned his smile. "Rosaleigh."

We crossed the street and I heard Julian call after us. "Nice to meet you, Rosaleigh." When we had almost reached the gate to my courtyard, I turned to look at my friend. "Oh, Jahane, he was really sexy, don't you think," I said breathlessly, at the recollection of almost being knocked down by the Greek God in the Quarter.

Jahane's springy curls bobbed up and down and she licked her lips. "He was, Rosie, and let me tell you, I think he was certainly into you."

"Pffttt, how would you know, you were too busy dragging me away." I smiled at the thought of the tall stranger; his long hair brushing along my cheek as he stopped me from falling on the ground, his strong hands gripping my waste and how they braced around my back to catch me. A small sigh escaped as the memory played over and over in my head.

"Ahem!" I looked up when Jahane cleared her throat and I quickly changed the subject.

"Jahane, let's head inside the shop and see if Mama has any new items. You know how she loves her trinkets and spell books." I air quoted and sprinted the few steps through the courtyard and through the back door of the shop.

We linked our arms and walked through the front of the shop. Sitting behind the counter was Miss Alina; the sign to the shop was propped up next to the counter. "What's the sign doing inside?" I asked.

Miss Alina looked up from her work and smiled. "Hello to you too, Rosie."

Heat spread across my cheeks and I walked around the counter to hug her. "I am sorry, Miss Alina, how are you?"

I glanced back down at the familiar sign that hung in front of the shop; the curly q's spelling out the words 'The Magic Crystal'. I turned at the sound of Miss Alina's voice. "It fell this morning, but thankfully didn't hit anyone," she said.

Miss Alina noticed Jahane standing behind me and smiled. "How's ya mama?" she asked.

"Oh, Mama is just fine; she's helping my auntie down the street," she replied.

"Jahane, do you think one of your brothers could come by the shop and rehang the sign?"

"Yes ma'am. I'll call Mama and ask her. I'm sure she will send one over right away."

As Jahane went off to call her mom, I bounced from foot to foot in anticipation. "Where is Mama?"

Miss Alina's eyebrows crooked at me over the glasses. "She is upstairs."

"Thank you." I turned and ran past Jahane as she was hanging up the phone. She followed me outside and up the steps two at a time. "Mamaaaa, Mamaaa" I hollered, through the house.

My mother came around the corner from the kitchen, wiping her hands on a dishtowel. "What is it, my dear?"

I stopped and looked at her. "Oh, Mama, I met a guy today, didn't I, Jahane?" I turned around to see my best friend enter and nod her head.

"You did?" She questioned as she ushered us both into the kitchen. "You two come sit and have some sweet tea and tell me all about this new guy." Her mouth quirked into a smiled as we all traipsed into the kitchen.

We both sat, and as Mama brought us two glasses of tea, my words tumbled out of my mouth. Between breaths, I took a few sips of my tea. "Ask Jahane, I played it very cool like I wasn't interested. Besides, Jahane was dragging me down the street as he was talking." I laughed and flipped my hair over my shoulder. I looked over at Jahane and she stuck her tongue out at me. Even at her age, she still sometimes acted childish. I nudged her. "Come on, you know it was true."

"Yeah, yeah, but you know if I hadn't dragged you away ya'll would have continued to make googly eyes at each other."

I rolled my eyes and turned back to my momma.

"So, honey, what is this mystery man's name?" she asked, as she pulled out her chair and sat.

With a dreamy sigh, I breathed out "His name is Julian."

My mother quirked a brow at me, "Julian, is it?"

"Yes, Mom, and he is dreamy." I cupped my face in my hands and sighed.

She placed her hands on the table and stood. I glanced down at them, and noticed how similar in size and shape they were to my own. As she pushed her chair back in, she looked at us and asked.

"Jahane, would you like to stay for dinner?"

"Sure, Miss Magnolia, I'll call my mom and let her know."

I turned to Jahane as my mom cooked us dinner. "So, do you really think he was into me?"

She leaned in closer and whispered in my ear, "Bestie, if he could have taken you right there on the street, he would have."

My mother gasped and shook her spoon at her. "Jahane, please refrain from being so uncouth."

"I'm sorry, yes ma'am." She hung her head, but looked up at me under her lashes and grinned like the Cheshire cat. We both erupted into a fit of giggles. I caught my mom staring at us and it caused even more laughter.

⚜⚜⚜⚜

The next morning the sun filtered through a crack in my curtains. I popped an eye open and groaned. Reluctantly, I scooted out of the warm bed, and as my feet touched the cold, hardwood floors, I got a small chill. My bare feet slapped along the floor as I walked over to the window. When I yanked the curtains open, the warmth danced in and the heat warmed me instantly. My mood lightened and I felt the corners of my lips tug into a smile. The streets were already crowded with tourists and interspersed with locals lugging their instruments down to the corner. Down below I saw the guy from yesterday. His long hair was pulled up and away from his face, showing off a strong jawline. Just as I was about to open the window to call out to him, my mother's voice broke into my thoughts.

"Coming, Mama." I stuffed my feet into a pair of slippers and ran down the hall. I turned the corner swiftly to see her singing in front of the kitchen stove. I stood in the archway, leaned against the wooden frame, and watched. Suddenly, the lilting tune made my feet move and I floated into the kitchen. My laugh echoed though the kitchen and my mother turned to face me.

"Ah, Rosie, there you are. How would you like to help me make bread pudding?"

I beamed at her and my head shook excitedly. "Of course I would, Mama."

"All right, Petal, get the French bread from the pantry. But, not the new one."

I headed off to the pantry and opened the door. My eyes scanned the shelves and found the two-day-old French bread. On my way out, I had a fabulous idea and grabbed a bottle of red wine.

"Mama, how about some wine?" I held the bottle up and shook it, then bounced out with the bread snuggled in my arm.
She shook her head at me and laughed. "Oh, Rosie, I don't know."

"Oh, come on, Mama. Let's have some fun."

"All right, but just one bottle." She cocked an eyebrow at me as she uncorked the bottle. The cork flew across the room and spun on the floor until it settled. I burst out laughing. She pulled two wine glasses out of the cabinet and poured us each a glass.
"Thank you, Mama." We clinked glasses, then I swirled the drink in the glass and took a sip. The smooth liquid slid down my throat. I licked my lips and placed my glass down. "Ok, Mama, let's get to baking." I giggled and lifted myself up onto the counter and swung my legs back and forth.

"Rosie, you are such a light weight." She laughed and grabbed the bread and a knife.

I laughed and took another sip of my wine. My mother's steady hands chopped up the bread into little cubes. Once all the bread was placed into the bowl and the milk covered it, making it a thick mixture, she placed it on the middle shelf in the fridge. Her slender hand picked up the glass and she drank her wine.

"So, Rosie, when will you see this Julian again?"

"I'm not sure, but I did see him walking around the Square this morning." I wondered if he had been searching for me. After all, I didn't give him anything, but my name. Suddenly, I thought *oh no, what if I never saw him again.*

She took the mixture out of the fridge and we finished making the desert. Thirty minutes passed and we erupted into a fit if hysterical giggles. My mama lifted her hand and music filled the room. I cocked a brow at her.

"Just go with it, Rosie." She danced around the kitchen, her voice belting out the song that flowed magically though the house. I sat on the counter, sipping my wine.

"Come on, Rosie, dance with me." She grabbed my hand and I jumped off the counter. She spun me around and around the kitchen. We bopped around with glasses in hand, laughing and clinking our glasses as we headed through the apartment, singing.

We plopped on the sofa from all the excitement, careful not to spill our drinks. I heard the timer on the oven ding and I jumped up and walked back into the kitchen. "Hurry, Mama."

Once the bread pudding was done, my mom took it out of the oven and cut two squares. She gently placed them on plates and poured the rum sauce all over. As we sat down, I cut into my dessert. "Mama..." I started.

"What's wrong, Petal?"

"Nothing really." I continued to play with my food.

"Come on tell me, sweetie."

"It's just, what if, I mean, oh it's silly. But what if I see Julian again and he sees the real me. Scars and all."

"Oh dear," she scooted her chair closer to me and grabbed my hands and held them in hers. "If he doesn't like you for who you are then he's not worth it, right?"

I nodded and hugged her. "You are the best mama ever."

"Besides, who wouldn't love you for the beautiful flower that you are. You, my dear Petal, are an amazing person."

"Thank you, Mama. You always know how to make me feel better."

"As your mom, that's my job."

I nodded and finished eating my bread pudding, enjoying every sweet bite. After I was done, I got up to put my plate in the sink. "Mama, thank you for today. I think I may head over to Jahane's for a while. There's still a little daylight left."

"Have fun, my beautiful Petal." As I left the kitchen, I heard my mom singing.

True beauty shines not of the skin but the heart. And love never ending should be true from the start.

Through magic and wisdom let true nature show, to give all that seek the knowledge to know. Guidance and love to let a bond build, For hearts and souls forever to be filled.

I shook my head as I headed down the steps and off to my best friend's house. When I reached her little shotgun house I walked up the cement steps and knocked on the door. Mrs. Kellete opened the door. "Hello, Rosie, how are you today?"

"I'm great, ma'am. Is Jahane here?"

"No, dear, she is down the street helping her grandma. You may go over there if you'd like."

"Yes ma'am, but I know how she values her time with her grandma. Let her know I stopped by please."

"I will, be careful going back home." She shut the door and I ascended the steps and headed towards Jackson Square.

The Square was bustling with tourists and artists. I stepped around dozens of people and headed to Café Dumonde. As I crossed the street a man tipped his hat and smiled at me. I returned the smile and headed into the busy café. Waiting at the window, I ordered a café au lait. With my coffee in hand, I made my way back across the street. The man from before was perched on his little carriage, his mule waiting patiently for the next tour. I hesitated slightly and then crossed the street quickly, the pain from my accident still fresh in my mind. I sipped my coffee and entered the square. Finding an empty bench I sat down. This was my favorite time of the day, right before the artist's picked up their work, and the partying started. After about an hour of people watching, I decided to head home.

When I entered the apartment it was quiet. I'm sure Mama was somewhere, but I was tired so I went to my bedroom. After changing into my pj's, I slipped into my bed and curled up under the soft confines of my quilt. Soon, I fell fast asleep and.

I walked through the crowded streets of New Orleans. As I looked up, I saw that the sky was clear of clouds, so I headed toward Jackson Square. When I stepped up the concrete steps and entered the square, in a flash, all the people dispersed, except for one. His back was to me, but I was pulled towards him. Slowly walking towards this mystery man, I was suddenly nervous. He turned to face me and I gasped.... it was Julian. He walked up to me and took me in his arms.

The next morning I woke with a renewed sense of hope. Opening the door to the balcony, I stepped out and saw what a beautiful day it will turn out to be. I knew I had to enjoy this glorious day. I went back inside and headed to the closet. Quickly, I grabbed a long skirt and a pink peasant shirt and got dressed. As I ran through the house, I stopped long enough to jot down a note to my mom, since I knew she was still sleeping.

When I stepped outside and headed down the steps, the sunlight was bright and danced across the courtyard. The flowers instantly perked up and opened up to the sky. I picked one of the wild flowers and tucked it behind my ear. As I walked down the street, I decided to step into the grocery store across the street. Once inside, I went straight over to the fruits and vegetables.

"Ma'am, how are the melons this time of year?" I heard a voice I recognized, but decided to play it cool.

I slowly turned around to see Julian holding up a melon. I tried to feign ignorance of who he was, so I cocked my head and smiled at him.

"Do you not recognize me?" he asked.

I knew it was time to give in. "Oh, hello Julian, it's nice to see you again." Knowing it would be fun to mess with him, I asked. "Is that the best pick up line you have?" He placed his hand over his heart, feigning hurt, and then burst out laughing.

"Rosie, how would you like to take a walk with me? You know, to get to know each other."

I took the melon he still had in his hand and placed it among the others. I felt a slight heat cross my face, but grabbed his hand anyway. "Let's go." There was no way in hell I was going to let this one get away again.

As we walked down the cobblestone street, he gripped my hand. I almost burst with excitement. We passed an outside café and he looked at me. "Are you hungry, Rosaleigh?"

I nodded as my stomach let out a fierce growl, remembering I'd skipped breakfast and I laughed from embarrassment. "Yes, I am starving."

He placed his hand on my back and ushered me to a small, round table in the back. He pulled my chair out for me and I sat. *Wow, he's even a gentleman. His momma must have raised him right* I thought to myself.

A young man walked over to the table and I smiled up at him. "What would you like to drink?" he asked us.

"I'd like a sweet tea."

"Same for me," Julian said, as he looked over to me. I sunk into my chair as his eyes bored into me, his long brown hair cascaded down his shoulders. Oh, how I longed to run my fingers through those locks. Regaining my composure, I spoke up. "Julian, tell me more about you?"

His smile broadened his features. "What would you like to know?"

"Everything," I blurted out.

He laughed and leaned across the table and grabbed my hand that had been fiddling with the napkin. "Well let's see, I'm from Terrebonne Parish. My family owns a sugarcane plantation that has been in the family for as long as I can remember. Unfortunately, my father died when I was young so it's been only my mother and me. I took over the business when I was old enough. But when she died I moved out here to get away. I left the business in our lawyer's control."

Before I could ask him a question, the waiter came over and placed two glasses of tea down. "Are ya'll ready to order?"

I hurriedly flipped open the menu. "I'll have a cheese omelet with mushrooms."

As Julian placed his order, I watched the way his lips moved and hoped this impromptu date would end with his lips on mine. *Good gracious, I've been hanging out with Jahane for way too long.* I grinned at the thought of what she would say when she found out I was on a date with Julian.

"What are you smiling at?" The sexy Cajun lilt that pulled me from my thoughts had me sinking into my chair.

"Nothing," I picked up my tea and sipped.

"Now, Rosaleigh, your turn," he cocked a brow at me, "have you always lived here in the city?"

"My mother and I moved out here when I was eight. I'm also from a small bayou town like you, and lost my dad as well, though I was a baby and don't remember him."

He gripped my hand and caressed it. "I'm so sorry, Rosaleigh."

"It's all right. Let's discuss something else."

"Anything you want to talk about?"

"Sure what is it that you do Julian, since you no longer run a sugar cane plantation?"

He laughed. "Rosie I work offshore as an underwater diver."

"Oh, that sounds dangerous." I became concerned.

He reached across the table and grabbed my hand. “Rosie are you worried about me?” He joked.

I shook my head. “Nah I’m....” I was interrupted by the waiter placing our plates of food on the table.

“This looks delicious,” I said to waiter with a smile.

He nodded and turned around, leaving us to eat.

⚜⚜⚜⚜

After we finished our meal, he walked me back to my apartment. We walked through the courtyard hand in hand. “Rosaleigh, I would love it if I could have another date with you.”

Before I could answer him, my momma walked out of the shop. Her smile was a knowing one. “Hello, Rosie, who is this?” She winked at me, followed by a motherly smile.

“Mom, this is Julian.” I beamed up at her.

Julian reached out his hand. “Hello, Miss Delacroix, it’s nice to meet you.”

She took his offered hand. “It’s nice to meet you as well. I’ll let you two say goodbye. I need you to run the shop for a couple of days. I have to take a trip.” At my expression, she leaned down to me. “No worries, my Petal, I just have something to take care of.”

I nodded, as she kissed me goodbye and headed to the apartment. “Love you, Mama.”

“I love you too, Petal. Be good to my daughter, Julian.”

He quirked a brow at me, as if saying, *so I must have gotten the green light to date you.* “All right, Rosaleigh, I must be getting back to work. Maybe I can see you later tonight?”

“Sure, I would love that.”

Before he left, he leaned down and placed a small kiss on my lips. The moment his lips touched mine, a spark flowed through me. “I’ll see you later then.”

I nodded and watched him walk away.

Bread Pudding with Rum Sauce

Bread pudding is by far one of the best deserts we have here in Louisiana. I used this one for Magnolia to teach Rosie because Magnolia knew that Rosie would fall in love with Julian. This recipe in other words, is magic.

Makes 1 “half-pan” (10”x12” and 2” deep)

Ingredients for Bread Pudding

10 eggs
1 quart granulated sugar
1 quart half and half
1 Tbsp. vanilla extract
1 Tbsp. ground cinnamon
Pinch of salt
2.5 loaves (30” each) day-old French bread

Ingredients for Rum Sauce

½ lb. light brown sugar
¼ lb. (or 8 Tbsp.) chilled butter- cubed
2 Tbsp. light corn syrup
1 tsp. ground cinnamon
Pinch of salt
½ cup rum

¼ cup cream

Yield: Makes 8-10 servings.

Bourbon Sauce:

In a saucepan, melt butter; add sugar and egg, whisking to blend well. Cook over low heat, stirring constantly, until mixture thickens. (Do not allow simmering, or it may curdle.) Whisk in bourbon to taste. Remove from heat. Whisk before serving. The sauce should be soft, creamy, and smooth.

Preparation Bread Pudding:

Preheat oven to 350°F.
Soak the bread in milk in a large mixing bowl. Press with hands until well mixed and all the milk is absorbed. In a separate bowl, beat eggs, sugar, vanilla, and spices together. Gently stir into the bread mixture. Gently stir the raisins into the mixture.

Pour butter into the bottom of a 9x13 inch baking pan. Coat the bottom and the sides of the pan well with the butter. Pour in the bread mix and bake at 350°F for 35-45 minutes, until set. The pudding is done when the edges start getting a bit brown and pull away from the edge of the pan. Can also make in individual ramekins.

Serve with bourbon whiskey sauce on the side; pour on to taste. Best fresh and eaten the day it is made.

A Magnolia Tree

2013... age twenty-six

It had been three days since my momma had disappeared and the hope I would see her again dissipated with each hour that passed. The cops had not tried really hard to find her, saying she probably ran off with some man. Which I knew was not possible.

As I sat on the sofa, I placed my head in my hands and replayed the last dream I'd had before her disappearance. It scared the hell out of me. I wondered what in the hell it all meant. Suddenly, my cell phone rang, and with a quick, glance I shook my head and ignored it. Within seconds, the phone beeped, alerting me to a text. Through tears, I saw it was from Jahane. *Where are you? Why are you not answering your phone?*

The tears rolled down my cheeks like an avalanche. After a few moments, I knew I had to do something to get my mind on something else. I stood and went into the kitchen to make breakfast. I opened the fridge and saw the milk and eggs, but when I grabbed the milk, my hands trembled and the carton crashed to the floor. Milk splattered all over the hardwood floor. Instantly, my tears poured out and I spoke to the empty kitchen, "Mama, where are you?" Even though I was alone, I expected to hear her voice in response. With a towel in my hand, I knelt down to clean up the mess. After I'd finished cleaning, I stood up, threw the empty milk carton in the trash, and tossed the wet towel in the sink. As I stood and contemplated making 'lost bread', I sighed loudly. I couldn't do it, I just couldn't do it. I needed to find my mama.

I grabbed my purse and headed outside. My pace quickened as the Square came into view. The closer I got to the shop belonging to my mama's best friend and confidant, my heart almost stopped. I passed all the tourists and artists in a blur. When I reached the front door of Miss Alina's shop, I caught my breath and wiped my tear stained face. As I stepped inside the posh interior, the bell tingled above the door. Miss Alina's head popped up at the noise. When she looked at me, her face full of concern, it made me burst into hysterical sobs.

"Oh dear child, what's wrong?" Her embrace comforted me like a warm blanket.

In-between hiccups I managed to speak, "Mama is gone. I...don't...know where... she...went." I slumped down and Miss Alina held me up.

"Rosie, Rosie, my dear, sweet child, please calm down. Come on; let's get some hot tea inside you." She held me tight and ushered me into the back of her shop.

Miss Alina went over to the counter where her little silver tea set was. From the sofa, I watched her grab a little cup with beautiful painted roses on it. (She used these only for me since they were my
favorite.) A floral scent wafted through the room as the tea bag hit the hot water. Miss Alina walked over with the little tray and sat down.

"Sugar, lemon, and honey, dear?"

My head nodded up and down in a slight move at her question. She took a little sugar cube and plopped it into my tea without even a splash. She squeezed a bit of honey and lemon in my cup. When she handed me the cup, I noticed a little white rose made from the sugar, with a yellow honey stem, floating on the top of my tea. I thought to myself, *I'm going crazy.* I blinked and it turned to a teardrop in a myriad of colors. I blinked again and the sugar and honey dissolved.

"Thank you, Miss Alina."

"You are welcome, Rosie, now drink up and rest. I'll be back, I hear a customer up front."
I sipped my tea; the smooth honey flowed down my throat and instantly calmed me. As I took another sip, silky flower petals gently tickled my nose. I pulled back from the cup and stared at my tea in fascination. Once again, I saw the rose, but this time it was a soft pink. I shook my head. *Now I've lost my mind. Oh, holy crap, I am going crazy.*

"No, Rosie, you aren't. Now go to sleep, dear. I'll never leave you." My mother's voice floated around in my head. With heavy lids, my eyes fluttered shut, opened again, and then shut as I drifted off to sleep.

⚜⚜⚜⚜

I stood in a field full of multicolored flowers, the air lingering with a hint of honey and lemon. The soft grass blades tickled my feet as I walked towards the flowers. When I stood in the middle of the blooms, my fingertips brushed over each soft petal. Off in the distance, an assortment of different shades of roses danced as their stems blew in the wind. The roses called out to me, so I ran over towards them. The aroma was subtle, but as I stepped closer, the scent grew stronger. I bent down to smell a soft, pink rose and the velvety petals brushed against my nose and cheek. I jumped back in astonishment.

"Rosie, Rosie." The soft melodic voice drifted through the air to settle in my ears. I glanced around the vast area and noticed a lone magnolia

tree off in the distance. Tiny birds flew above the tree; their wings fluttering in the breeze, chirping in sing song tones.

I glanced over my shoulder at the roses once more and smiled as they waved back and forth to me. Without hesitation, I walked over towards the giant tree. Upon a closer look, the beautiful white flowers began to turn brown until they disappeared into ashes and sprinkled down around me. I coughed and choked as they covered me. I looked up at the tree through the dust and noticed a single, white magnolia high above. I wiped off my dress, reached a hand up, and climbed the tree. The branches reached out and helped me in my descent. Each one seemed to take extra care with me, pushing me up and up until I was facing the lone flower. When I reached the flower, I plucked it from its branch. I held it gently in my hands and sniffed its sweet aroma. The petals tickled my nose. I brushed the flower along my cheek and it seemed to caress my face. I pulled it away and my fingers stroked each downy petal, which slowly began to turn brown. Each petal broke off and turned to dust, but as my fluorescent teardrops touched each remaining petal, they breathed life into each one. One by one, they floated high above me and swirled in dancing movements into the clouds. When I looked down at my hand, one single velvety petal fluttered up and down and rested in my hand.

From my spot in the tree, I pocketed the petal and noticed a figure off in the distance. In a blur, the cloaked figure hovered inches from my face. I screamed and the air whooshed around me……

⚜⚜⚜⚜

My eyes jerked open to see Miss Alina rocking back and forth in a chair, her expression littered with worry.

"Rosie, you must go home and pack and leave the city now." She prodded me.

"But…but…I must find my mama."

"Later, Rosie. Please go home and get as far away as you can from here. I know you've had a dream; it will come for you if you don't hide."

Shock plastered my face at the mention of my dream. "You know about it?"

"Not now, dear, I'll explain later. Your mother wants you to be protected. She has planned ahead for you. Come back only when you feel safe and you will know when that is."

"But what about Jahane and Julian?"

"They will understand and be here for you when you do return." She pushed me gently out the door.

⚜⚜⚜⚜

Later in my room, I pulled the heavy suitcase out of my closet. I tried to stifle my tears, but had no luck. Tears cascaded down my cheeks to fall on my folded clothes inside the suitcase. My eyesight blurred by numerous tears, I slowly pulled the zipper closed and wiped my eyes with the back of my hand. I plopped down on my bed next to my closed suitcase and looked around at my room for what I hoped wasn't the last time. My hand rested on the quilt and traced the stitching on each soft, colorful square. The loving memory of my mother sewing it flooded into my head. I stood up from the bed and walked over to the closet. In the back of the closet was a box that I held close to my heart. I reached in and took the folded up letter I'd found on the counter the day my momma left. My hands trembled as I gently unfolded the rumpled piece of paper. Without reading the letter, I refolded it and shoved it back into the box. I shook my head; it was still too soon to read the last words ever written by my mama.

Winds to blow and fire to burn.
Lessons you seek, your heart to learn.
Strength you will need, find deep inside.
Lean on these words to help you and guide.
Rely on the powers and love that surrounds,
And the true destiny you seek shall be found.

My heart pressed against my chest with the pain of my loss. I picked up my suitcase and headed through the hallway to the kitchen. I scribbled a quick note to Jahane and Julian, and then left my home and life in New Orleans and all I knew. As I closed the door, I swear I heard my mama's voice.

LOST BREAD

This French toast recipe, or pain perdu, is an easy preparation of thickly sliced bread soaked in a sweetened, vanilla-scented custard mixture and then fried in butter to golden perfection. The name, pain perdu, literally means lost bread, and is used in reference to using day-old bread that would otherwise be lost. Dress up this French toast recipe with a dusting of confectioners' sugar, whipped cream, or fresh berries.

Ingredients:

4 eggs
4 tablespoons granulated sugar
1 tablespoon vanilla extract
1 1/3 cups milk
8 thick slices of day-old bread, cut on a bias
4 tablespoons butter
Whipped cream, powdered sugar, or berries for garnish

Preparation

Beat the eggs, sugar, and vanilla extract together until the mixture is completely blended and smooth. Stir the milk into the egg mixture until it is fully incorporated. Place the slices of bread into the egg mixture, turn them over to coat all the surfaces, and allow the bread to soak for 10 minutes.

Melt 1 tablespoon butter in a large skillet set over medium heat. Cook 2 slices of soaked bread in the melted butter for 3 minutes. Turn the slices of French toast over and cook them for an additional 3 minutes, until they are golden brown and lightly crispy on each side. Repeat with the remaining butter and soaked bread.

This pain perdu recipe makes 4 servings.

Voodoo Vows

Voodoo Vows
Ghosts from the Past

The Guardians

Bred by Magic (The Guardians A Voodoo Vows Tail)

Coming Soon 2015

Gifted by Magic - The Guardians A Voodoo Vows Tail 2
Black Magic Betrayal - Voodoo Vows 2

About the Author

As a young girl, Diana Marie Dubois was an avid reader and was often found in the local public library. Now you find her working in her local library. Hailing from the culture filled state of Louisiana, just outside of New Orleans; her biggest inspiration has always been the infamous Anne Rice and her tales of Vampires. It was those very stories that inspired Diana to take hold of her dreams and begin writing. She is now working on her first series, Voodoo Vows.

Amazon Page: amazon.com/-/e/B00O97TWUO

Facebook: facebook.com/diana.m.dubois

Goodreads: goodreads.com/author/show/7690662

Instagram: instagram.com/dianamariedubois

Pinterest: pinterest.com/dianamdubois/

Twitter: twitter.com/DianaMDuBois

Website: www.dianamariedubois.com

Made in the USA
Columbia, SC
16 September 2022

67185636R00048